Published by English Heritage
23 Savile Row
London W1S 2ET

Copyright © authors, illustrator and English Heritage 2004

First published by English Heritage 2004

Edited by Val Horsler
Designed by Brian Shields, Design Systems
Printed in England by The Bath Press

ISBN 1 85074 877 2

C30, 3/04

Panic at the Roman Fort

A Cuthbert story

Nicky and Humphrey Welfare
Illustrations by Sue Shields

ENGLISH HERITAGE

'Come on Ben, bring Cuthbert,
I'll race you to that gate,'
shouted Anna.

Granny had taken Anna and Ben to see the remains of a fort built by the Romans a very long time ago. They had taken their bear, Cuthbert, with them.

'Is that all there is?' exclaimed Ben, a little disappointed.

'Granny, the Romans had proper buildings, didn't they?' asked Anna.

'Of course they did, dear,' said Granny. 'These have fallen down, that's all. Don't forget, they are nearly two thousand years old!'

It was very hot so they sat in the shade and Granny began to read
the guidebook to them.

Ben whispered to Anna, 'I wish we could see the fort as it really was.
It must have been an amazing place.'

Cuthbert winked. 'I can show you,' he said. 'Hold my paws tight.'

Suddenly the walls were much higher and the three of them were standing inside the fort in front of two tall towers. The enormous wooden gates of the fort were open.

'Let's go up to the top!' said Anna.

From the top they could see all of the buildings in the fort. 'What's that noise?' said Ben, turning round. 'It sounds just like our school football team walking across the playground.'

'Don't be silly!' said Anna. 'The Romans didn't play football!'

'No,' replied Cuthbert. 'But they did have studs on their sandals. Look! Some soldiers are coming. Let's go down and watch.'

Anna, Ben and Cuthbert stood and watched as the soldiers marched in.
They were followed by many more who were riding horses.
'Look at the one at the front with the bear skin on his head!' said Ben.
'Ah, yes!' said Cuthbert. 'It means that he is very important. Bears are, you
know. He's carrying the Standard which is rather like a special flag.'
'He looks very hot and tired,' said Anna. 'He has a sore, sunburnt nose.
Poor man, he needs sun cream, a proper sun hat and a drink of water.
He must be boiling in that uniform.'

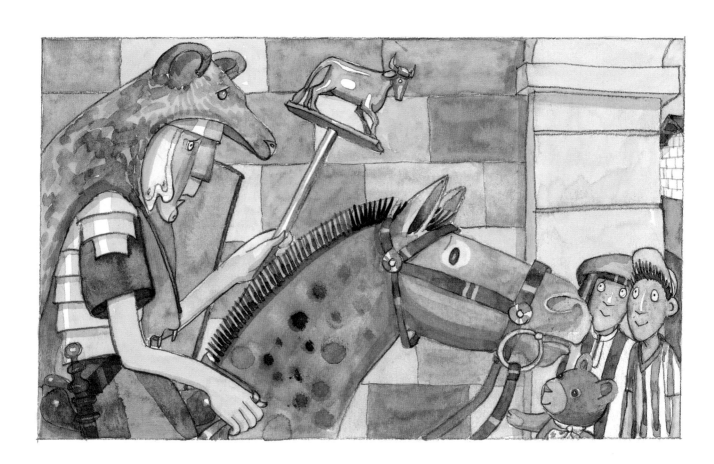

'Cuthbert, do all the soldiers come from Rome?' asked Ben as he
watched them coming in through the gate.
'No,' said Cuthbert. 'They come from many different countries.
Come on, you two, we've been standing here a long time. Let's go
and see the barracks where the soldiers live.'

They came to a long building with lots of doors. One of the doors was open. They peeped inside.

'There's no-one here at the moment. Is this a soldier's bedroom?' asked Anna.

'Oh no, eight soldiers share a little room at the back,' said Cuthbert. 'Here by the door they eat, talk and clean their kit.'

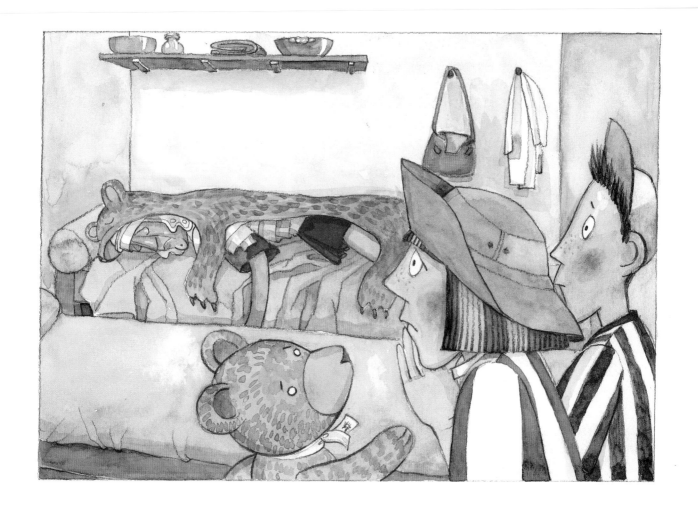

When they went further in they saw the Standard Bearer lying in a heap
on his bed, looking very sick.

Anna whispered to Cuthbert, 'He's gone a funny colour. Perhaps he's ill.
Shall I go and ask him if he's okay?'

'No, Anna, you and Ben wait by the door. I'll go and see what's wrong,'
said Cuthbert.

'Are you alright?' enquired Cuthbert. 'What's your name?'

'I'm Marcus, but ohh… my head hurts. I'm feeling so ill and dizzy. I even thought that you were a bear.'

'We liked the Standard that you were carrying,' said Cuthbert, trying to cheer him up.

'The Standard! What did I do with it? I can't remember. Have I lost it? OH NO! OH HELP! I must go and find it. WHAT WILL I DO? PL-E-A-SE HELP ME! I'll get into terrible trouble.'

'Perhaps we can help,' said Cuthbert to Anna and Ben. 'He should have put the Standard in the chapel, inside the headquarters. That's where they always keep them. Let's go!'

Cuthbert led them to the headquarters, which was the largest building in the fort, and then into the chapel.

'It's not here! Oh yikes! Where now, Cuthbert?' asked Ben.

'Er…' groaned Marcus.

'It could be in the strong-room, I suppose,' replied Cuthbert. 'That's where they keep all the money. It would be safe there.'

He went down the steps and opened the big thick door of the strong-room.

'It's not here,' whispered Anna, peering round behind Cuthbert.

'Er…' groaned Marcus.

Ben whizzed out of the building and went to the next one.

Marcus struggled after them.

'Not there!' shouted Cuthbert. 'That's the Commander's house.'

They ran on, and looked out through a small gate.

'What's that building, Cuthbert?' asked Ben.

'It's the bath-house,' replied Cuthbert, 'where the rooms are very hot or cold, dry or steamy. The Romans always had special baths for their soldiers to relax in. Let's try there.'

'Er…' groaned Marcus behind them.

Anna, Ben and Cuthbert tiptoed into the changing room of the bath-house, where soldiers were sitting around talking and playing games.

'It's not here,' said Anna, looking round carefully.

'I'm off on a quest to find the lost Standard!' chuckled Ben, rushing off into the next room which was full of steam.

'AHA!' he cried.

'OH, NO!' said Ben.
'It's not the Standard.
It's a broom!'

Anna laughed, but Ben had disappeared again, towards the hot, dry room. Cuthbert got there first and looked in. 'It's not here either,' he called to Ben, who had already turned round and had gone. Ben was beginning to enjoy the hunt.

'Is it in the cold room?' suggested Anna. 'It could be freezing in there,' said Ben. Cuthbert went ahead and peeped in. 'No luck!' he gasped, shivering.

'Bother!' exclaimed Ben as he rushed outside. 'Come on. Let's try somewhere else.'

'Er…' groaned Marcus. 'I can't keep up with you.'

Anna and Ben ran back into the fort and over to another gate. They peered out. 'Ooof!' said Ben. 'What's all this?'
Cuthbert explained that it was the village outside the fort where the families lived. 'Look! They're playing marbles!' cried Ben, hoping to join in a game.

'Stop, Ben. Marcus keeps trying to say something. What's the matter?'
asked Cuthbert, turning to Marcus.
'Er …' said Marcus. 'I still feel awful, but I've been trying to tell you.
I didn't go to all those places. I felt too ill.'
Cuthbert thought about what they should do next. 'I know,' he said.
'Let's go back to where we first met you, Marcus.'

He led them back to the barracks where he whizzed into the back room, and threw himself, head first, onto the bed.

'Cuthbert! What are you doing?' cried Anna. 'It can't be bedtime yet!'

'Got it!' cried Cuthbert, stretching his paw down between the bed and the wall.

'Thank you, thank you,' said Marcus. 'I must have dropped it when I felt so sick… I'll take it to the chapel NOW.'
'Well done, Cuthbert!' said Anna and Ben, laughing. 'Let's just make sure that he puts it in the chapel this time!'
'We have done our job here,' said Cuthbert. 'Hold my paws tight.'

Suddenly they were back on the rug with Granny. She was reading the last page of the guidebook.

'Granny, let's go and see the baths!' said Anna.

'And where they kept the money!' cried Ben.

'Oh you are good,' said Granny. 'You must have been listening very carefully.'

Cuthbert just smiled.

You can see for yourself the ruins of the Roman fort that Anna, Ben and Cuthbert visited with Granny. It is at Chesters, on Hadrian's Wall, where you can sit under the tree that they sat under, and where you can explore the gates of the fort, the barracks, the headquarters with its strong-room, and the bath-house where Ben thought that he had found the Standard.

The fort is in the care of English Heritage and is open every day of the year, except for three days at Christmas and on New Year's Day.

Not far away, near Newcastle, you can walk inside a full-size bath-house that has been built at Wallsend, and at South Shields you can see the gate of a fort.

A VIEW OF THE STRONG ROOM AT CHESTERS ROMAN FORT
PHOTOGRAPH: KEITH BUCK
© ENGLISH HERITAGE

ENGLISH HERITAGE

For more information about English Heritage,
or to become a member, please contact:

English Heritage Customer Services Department,
PO Box 569, Swindon SN2 2YP
telephone: 0870 333 1181; fax 01793 414926
e-mail: customers@english-heritage.org.uk

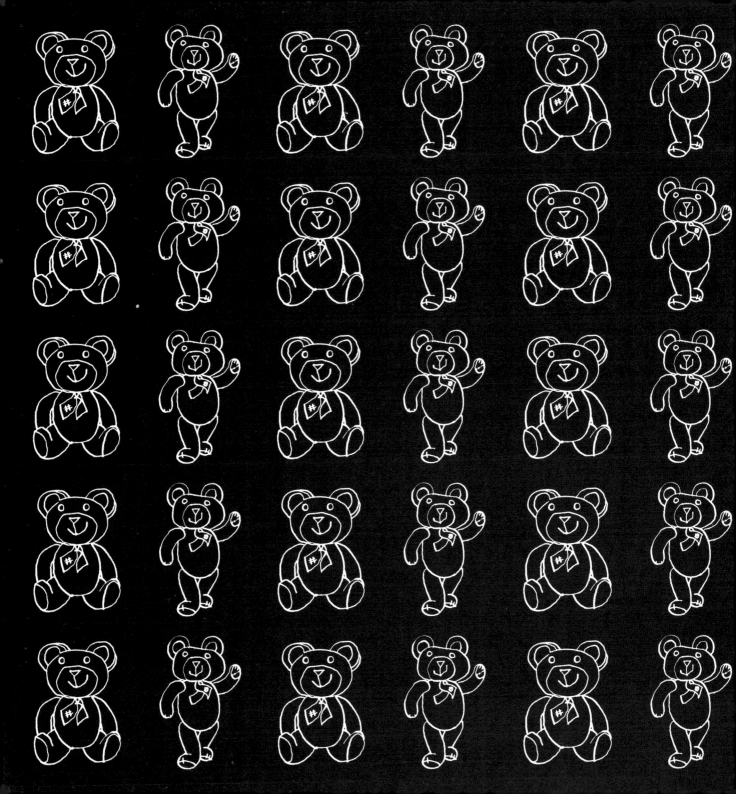